The Adventures of

Drippy
The Runaway Raindrop

by Sidney Sheldon
and Mary Sheldon

Illustrated by Alexandra Sheldon

DOVE KIDS

ISBN: 0-7871-0297-0

Printed in the United States of America

A Dove Kids Book
A Division of Dove Audio
8955 Beverly Boulevard
West Hollywood, CA 90048

Distributed by Penguin USA

First printing—September 1996

10 9 8 7 6 5 4 3

for
Elizabeth,
Rebecca,
Kimberly
and ALL the children of the world

2

Chapter One
Drippy

*T*his is a story about a raindrop. A very wonderful raindrop named Drippy.

Drippy was born on a foggy morning in the middle of a big meadow. He was cute and plump, and in him all the colors of the rainbow danced.

Drippy was born on a blade of grass. Now, because you are so much larger than a raindrop, a blade of grass seems very tiny to you. But to Drippy, that blade of grass was like a tall tree. And when it waved in the wind, it felt as scary and exciting to Drippy as being on a roller coaster ride would seem to you!

From the moment he was born, Drippy liked the feeling of being scared and excited. All of his brothers and sisters and cousins stayed obediently on their blades of grass. But Drippy kept dripping down to the ground. That is why his mother, Mrs. Dewdrop, named him Drippy.

"Drippy!" she scolded, when he had slid down the grass for the thirty-third time that morning, "You must stay up where it's safe!"

And for the thirty-fourth time, she lifted him back onto the blade.

But Drippy had no intention of staying there. The green meadow around him looked like a wonderful spooky forest and he wanted to explore.

"Mothers!" Drippy sighed. "They won't let you have any fun."

And as soon as Mrs. Dewdrop moved away to look after her other children, Drippy slid once more off his blade of grass.

"Whee!"

Kerplunk!

There he was on the ground. And while his mother's back was still turned, he rolled quietly off into the green meadow.

I've run away from home, Drippy thought proudly. *I'm the bravest raindrop that ever was!*

Drippy rolled happily along, exploring the new world, not even thinking about how sad and frightened his mother would be to find him gone. The only thing he cared about was having fun! And this was certainly fun!

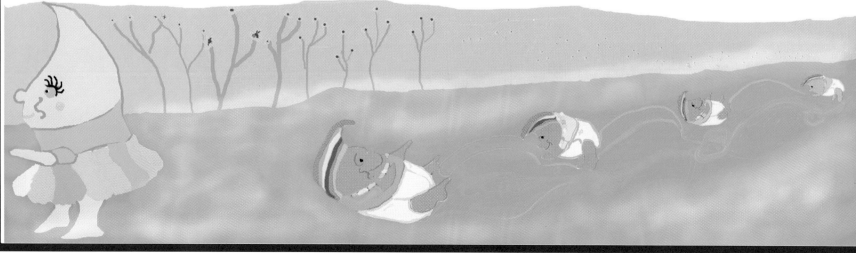

Drippy was so happy and proud of himself that he started to laugh. And when he laughed, he shook all over -- he was all water and rainbow, remember.

Suddenly, a deep voice next to him said, "What's so funny?" Drippy stopped laughing. The voice came from a huge green creature with big bulging eyes and two long waving horns on its head. It was a monster! "I'm going to die!" Drippy thought.

Chapter Two
Drippy & Leapy

Drippy stared at the monster, terrified.

You would be terrified, too, if you were a raindrop.

"Who are you?" asked Drippy.
"I'm Leapy, the grasshopper. You're a new raindrop aren't you?"

"Very new,"

Drippy said proudly.

"I was just born."

"Where's your family?" Leapy asked.
Drippy managed to look very sad.
"I don't have any family," he whispered.

This was, of course, a lie but Drippy was more interested in making up a good story than in telling the truth.

Leapy, who was a kind-hearted grasshopper, felt sorry for him.

"Well," he said, "I have a family. In fact, I was just on my way home to them. Perhaps you'd like to come along with me and have some breakfast with us."

"I'd love to!"

Drippy said,

excitedly.

What an adventure! Breakfast with a grasshopper! Drippy could just imagine himself telling his family all about it when he got home. Except he wouldn't tell it quite as it actually happened. No, it would be much more fun if he said that Leapy was a huge fire-breathing monster who had tried to kill him.

In his mind, Drippy practiced what he would say.

"This horrible monster came towards me. I couldn't even see the top of his head, it was so tall! Its tail thrashed and its teeth snapped. But was I scared? Of course not! I simply pulled up a sharp blade of grass and used it as a sword. And the monster was so terrified, it ran away."

Then he would smile modestly.

Yes, that's what he would say. And everyone would be so impressed.

Leapy lifted Drippy onto his scaly back. And then, with a tremendous bound, he jumped away towards home.

What a ride it was! Every time they leaped up, *boing!* Drippy felt stretched like a rubber band. And every time Leapy came down, *bang!* Drippy quivered all over. But it takes a lot to hurt a raindrop, so Drippy just laughed and had a wonderful time.

At last they landed in a little glade in the meadow. And there were Leapy's handsome family; a wife and ten children.

17

Drippy had a lovely time playing with the children. They took him for rides on their backs, and they performed a concert for him -- playing the beautiful music that grasshoppers can make by rubbing their hind legs together.

Drippy was very impressed -- and very jealous.

"I could play music like that if I wanted," he bragged.

He imagined himself standing on a big concert stage, bowing to an audience; the most famous musician in the world.

But the little grasshoppers only laughed.

19

"Playing this music is a special gift Nature gives to grasshoppers," they told him. "But you have your own special gift, Drippy. And yours is perhaps the most important one of all."

Drippy liked the sound of that.
"What is my special gift?" he asked.

But at that moment, before the little grasshoppers could answer, Leapy appeared.

"It's time I took Drippy back to where I found him," he said.

The little grasshoppers were sorry to see Drippy go. They hugged him with their feelers and told him to take care of himself. Drippy felt very proud because they liked him so much.

I must be very loveable, he thought. *In fact, I'm probably the most loveable raindrop in the world.*

And it never even occurred to him to say thank you to the little grasshoppers for the nice time they had given him.

Leapy put Drippy on his back, and once again they hopped over the meadows, until they were near the spot where they had first met.

Gently, Leapy put Drippy down. He looked rather worried. "Be careful, little raindrop," he said.
Drippy couldn't understand why Leapy looked so serious. After all, he was Drippy the great hero.
"Why should I be careful?" he asked.

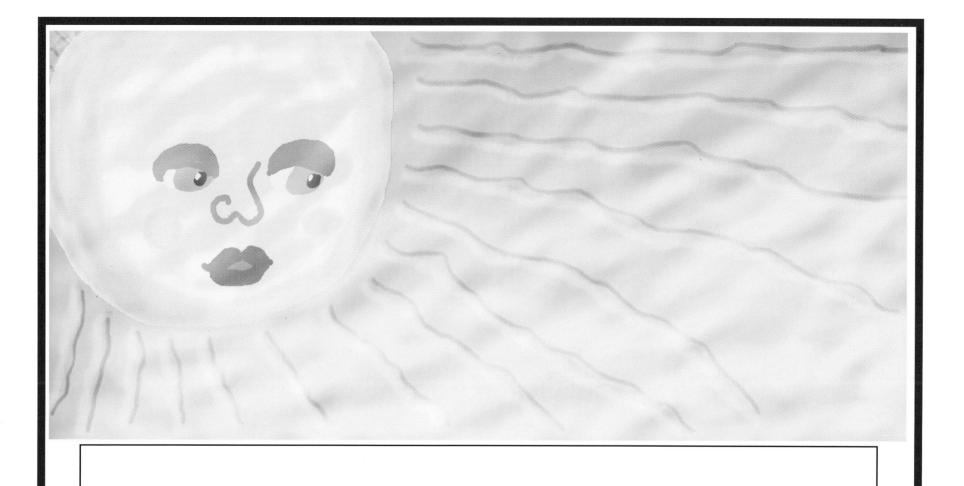

"The fog is lifting, and the sun is going to come out."

"What's the sun?" asked Drippy.

Leapy shook his head slowly.

"I thought everyone knew what the sun is. It's a big yellow grasshopper in the sky."

Drippy laughed,
"That doesn't scare me."

Leapy looked pityingly at Drippy.
"You don't understand, Drippy. He drinks raindrops."

Drippy's eyes opened very wide. He was the most loveable, the most heroic and the bravest raindrop in the world. And he certainly didn't want anyone drinking him!

"What should I do?" he asked.

"I'll hide you," Leapy said.

And he picked Drippy up and put him under a leaf high on a tree.

"There, you'll be safe here. The sun won't be able to find you. Just lie still, and don't come out till he's gone."

Drippy did not bother to say thank you. He was too busy imagining how he was going to describe his latest brave adventure when he got home -- about how he had killed the sun ...

"Goodbye," Leapy said. "Good luck!"

The grasshopper crouched down, gave a huge bound in the air, and disappeared into the green forest.

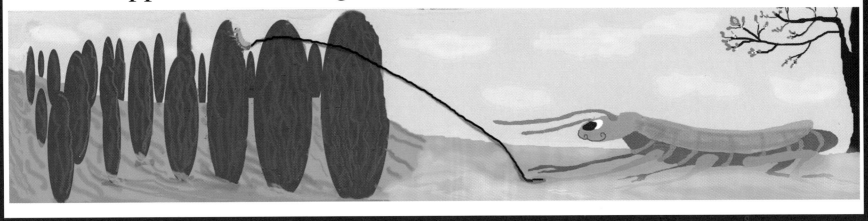

Drippy lay back on his leaf and daydreamed some more.

The leaf was very soft and comfortable and because of all the morning excitement he began to feel very sleepy. His eyes got heavier and heavier and soon they were closed. Drippy was asleep.

High up in the sky, the sun came out, strolling along the clouds.

Now, if there were no sun, nothing on earth would live. No grain would grow. No flowers would grow. There would be no day, only eternal night. So, to all the world, the sun is a great blessing. But not to raindrops!

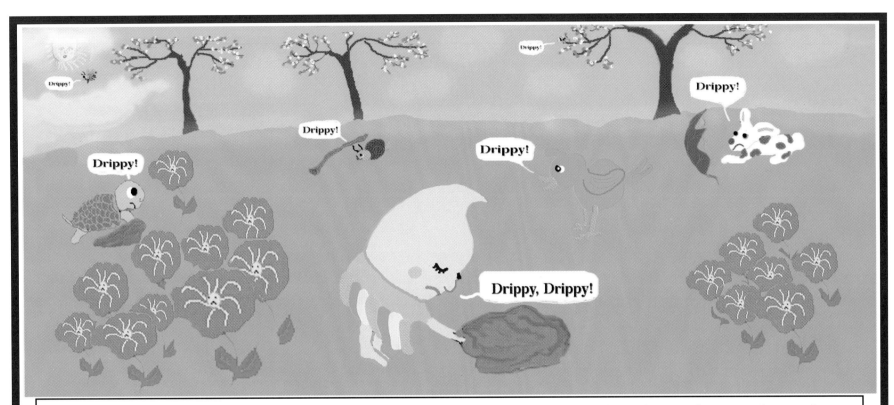

When Drippy's mother, Mrs. Dewdrop, looked up into the sky she quickly gathered up all her little raindrop children to hide them in the shade of a friendly oak tree. But she could not find Drippy. She looked everywhere. She looked under leaves and on tree trunks. She looked under twigs and stumps and stones. But there was not a sign of Drippy.   She called as loudly as she could in her little raindrop voice, "Drippy! Drippy!"

And the crickets took up the call, chirping, "Drippy! Drippy!"

And the bees heard them and began buzzing Drippy's name.

And all the birds began singing, "Drippy, Drippy!"

The whole meadow hummed with his name, but Drippy did not hear them. He was still sound asleep, dreaming and dreaming.

All over the meadow, it was getting hotter and hotter, as the sun grew stronger and stronger. He was very thirsty. Very thirsty. He drank at high rivers and great lakes and vast oceans and ponds. But still, he wanted a little dessert. And as he moved across the sky, he looked down and saw something glittering on a tree top. Could that be a raindrop? A fat little raindrop? The perfect way to end his meal!

He leaned closer so that he could get a better look.
He was going to drink Drippy!

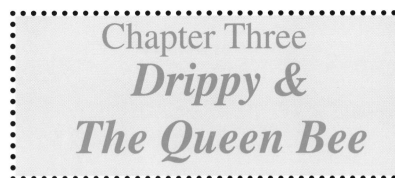

Chapter Three

Drippy & The Queen Bee

Just as the sun began to drink Drippy, Drippy woke up. *"I'm disappearing!"* he thought.

And at that very instant, there was a *buzz, buzz* over Drippy's head. A bee flew by.

This was not just an ordinary bee. This was a beautiful Queen Bee who ruled over all the other bees. And when she saw the sun looking thirstily at Drippy, she quickly spread her wings and flew down to the leaf where the little baby raindrop lay. Quickly, she picked Drippy up and flew away with him. *Buzz!*

The sun blinked, confused. The little light at the top of the tree was gone. So there was no plump raindrop -- he must have imagined it. Grumpily, the sun sighed and moved on.

Drippy was safe in the Queen Bee's arms, but he had no idea where he was, or who the strange creature was who was holding him.

"Who are you?" Drippy asked.

"I'm a bee," she said softly.

"What's a bee?"

"Me."

"What do bees do?"

The Queen Bee thought for a moment.

"We buzz."

She buzzed for him.

Drippy was not impressed.

"Is that all you do?"

"No, of course not," she laughed. "Bees pollinate flowers and make honey."

"What's honey?"

She was carrying some honey with her, and she gave Drippy a tiny taste.

"That's delicious!" Drippy cried, and then added quickly, "I could make honey too, if I wanted to."

The Queen Bee shook her head, smiling.

"Only bees can make honey," she told him. "You see, everything is put on this Earth for a special purpose. And each one of us has his or her own job to do."

"What's my job?" Drippy asked.

"Don't you know, little raindrop?"

"No."

"Well, you'll find out someday. But in the meantime, I'll tell you this -- you have one of the most important jobs on earth."

Just like Leapy's children had said!

So he truly was a special raindrop. Drippy grew more conceited than ever.

"Where can I take you?" the Queen Bee asked him. "Where does your family live?"

Drippy put on his saddest face. He told her the same lie he had told Leapy. "I have no family," he said.

The Queen Bee bent down and kissed him gently.

"I'm flying home to my family," she said. "Perhaps you'd like to come and spend a little time with us."

"I'd love to!" Drippy told her. A new adventure!

The Queen Bee flew with Drippy all over the meadow. Looking down, Drippy saw many wonderful things. Bright-colored flowers, hopping insects, rabbits and gophers playing on the moist green earth.

Drippy was interested in everything. The Queen Bee told him what each creature was, and then Drippy made up stories about them in his mind. And of course he was always the hero!

Soon he noticed that the Queen Bee was flying lower.

"Are we at your home yet?" Drippy asked.

"Yes," the Queen Bee said. "We have reached my hive."

For a moment Drippy couldn't imagine what a hive was -- all he could see was a strange large sort of sack attached to a tree. But the Queen took him inside -- and in a moment Drippy was in another world.

Have you every been inside a bee hive? I don't expect you have--but if you did, you would find it like the biggest, most organized office building in the world. When the Queen entered, all the bees stopped their work and bowed low before her.

She smiled graciously.

"We have a special guest," she said. "This is my friend Drippy." The bees also bowed to Drippy, and Drippy tried to bow back. But it is not easy for a raindrop to make a bow, and Drippy ended up by sliding halfway across the hive!

"Let me show you around," the Queen told Drippy.

The hive was filled with tiny six-sided cubicles, called honeycombs.

"What are they made of?" Drippy asked.

"Wax," the Queen said. "Our worker bees make wax from their own bodies to make the honeycombs."

Drippy was jealous. He wished he could make wax, too -- but he couldn't even make a bow!

"And what's inside the honeycombs?"

"Honey."

Drippy was impressed.

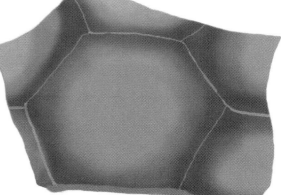

"How do you make honey?" he asked.

The Queen smiled.

"It's quite a job. And it all starts with flowers."

"In order to make one pound of honey, guess how many flowers we need?"

But Drippy had never been to school, and he didn't know how to count yet.

"Green?" he guessed.

The Queen laughed.

"No, green's a color."

"Wednesday?" Drippy guessed again.

The queen continued to laugh.

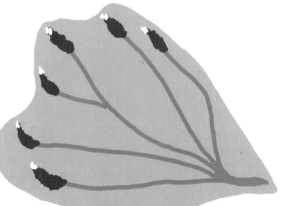

"No. Wednesday's a day of the week. The answer is three million flowers," she told him.

"That was going to be my next guess," Drippy told her.

Of course it wasn't, but Drippy didn't like to be wrong.

Drippy couldn't believe how busy the hive was. Everywhere he looked, different bees were doing different things.

"Some of them are worker bees," the Queen told him. "They are the ones who gather the honey, and make the honeycombs. Others are drones. They don't do much of anything, except tell jokes and make us laugh. And still others are nursemaids--they take care of the royal children."

Drippy was interested in the royal children.

"What do they do?"

"They grow and learn and have fun."

Just like me! Drippy thought happily. *Especially the having fun part!*

"Would you like to meet them?" the Queen asked.

"Yes," Drippy cried.

So the Queen took Drippy to the nurseries, and there were the royal princesses. At first Drippy felt a little shy. He tried his bow again, and this time he bent too far over and ended up turning a somersault! The princess bees started laughing, and soon they were all friends.

They all had a lovely visit together, playing games and eating so much honey that Drippy began to turn a pale yellow.

All too soon, the Queen Bee came to take Drippy away.

"I have some business in the meadow now," she said. "So I can take you back to where I found you."

The royal princesses kissed Drippy and told him they would miss him. He liked being kissed, and thought again, *I must be the most adorable raindrop in the world!*

But it did not occur to him to kiss them back, or even to say thank you for the nice time they had given him.

The Queen Bee picked up Drippy and flew with him back to the big green leaf.

"The sun's still out," she told him. "So you'd better be careful. I'm going to put you where you'll be safe."

And she flew over to a big yellow flower, and tucked
Drippy inside its petals. Then she kissed him goodbye.
"Good luck to you, baby raindrop," she said.

Drippy nodded. He didn't say thank you for the lovely afternoon, or for the honey, or for the rescue. No, Drippy was too busy to say thank you. He was too busy thinking of himself.

Thinking of himself, and all the great stories he would tell his mother and his father and his sisters and his brothers and his cousins when he got home.

"This wicked Queen Bee kidnapped me," he would say.
"She took me to her hive and held me prisoner there -- but I managed to escape ... I disguised myself as a big drop of honey, and when everyone's back was turned ..." And on and on.

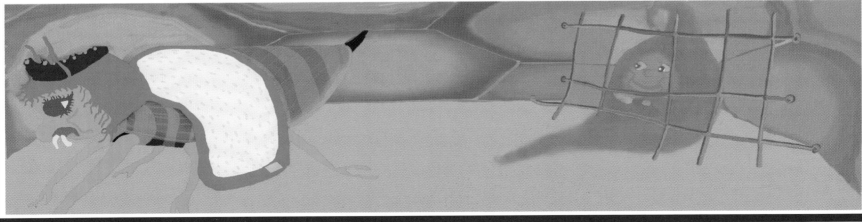

Drippy lay in the sweet-smelling flower for a long time, thinking about what a hero he was. Soon the sky began to get dark and night fell. Drippy had never seen night before. Remember, he had been born only that morning.

In the sky, the stars and the moon were out. Of course Drippy had no idea that they were stars and the moon. He thought they were bright lights put up just for him; just so that he could have a new adventure.

"Well, I'm ready!" Drippy said excitedly. And he sat up in the flower and looked around.

The movement attracted the attention of a little hummingbird on his way home from a party. Quickly, he swooped down to the flower where Drippy was. Drippy stared at the hummingbird, but he didn't feel at all afraid. He had seen so much that day that nothing could surprise him!

"What a strange-looking grasshopper you are!" he told the hummingbird with a yawn.

"I'm not a grasshopper at all," the hummingbird buzzed back.

"Well, you're an even stranger-looking bee!"

The hummingbird laughed.

"I'm not a bee either. I'm a hummingbird."

Another adventure to tell everyone about back home, Drippy thought proudly.

"Hello, hummingbird!" he said. "What do you do?"

The hummingbird smiled a long, slow smile at him. And he said in a very soft voice, "I drink raindrops."

And with that, he bent close to Drippy and began to drink him!

Chapter Four
Drippy &
The Wind

Far away, across the sea, the Wind was flying.

Now, the Wind is an amazing creature, with many amazing moods. When the Wind is in a mischievous mood, he loves to play. He blows against the sails of ships and sends them racing across the water. He rattles windows of tall office buildings, and blows napkins off outdoor tables. He blows newspapers in front of horses, and knocks hats off the heads of people crossing streets.

When the Wind is in an angry mood, he isn't so much fun to be with. When he blows really hard, cyclones and hurricanes happen, and buildings are knocked down, and automobiles are carried up into the air and ocean waves become as tall as mountains.

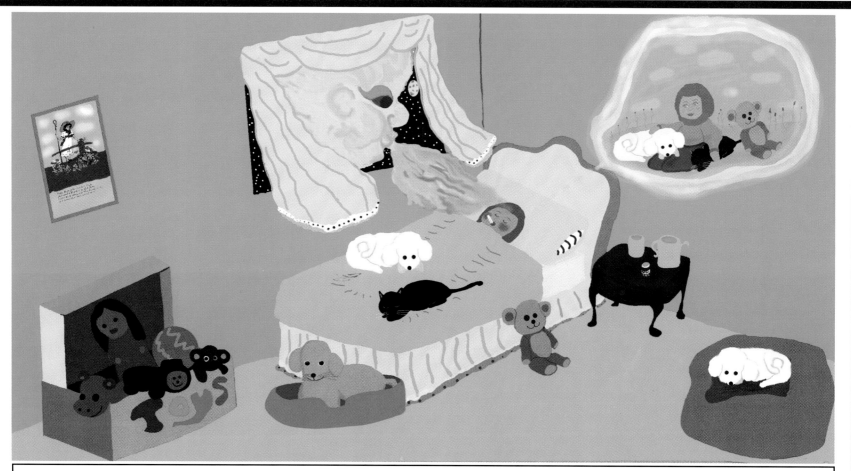

And then again, in other moods, the Wind can be very gentle and loving. He races around the world doing nice things. He cools the heads of children with hot fever, and sends them dreams of health. In farm countries, he turns the windmills that grind grain to feed hungry people.

It was Drippy's good luck that the Wind happened to be passing over the flower just at the moment when the humming-bird was starting to drink him. And it was also Drippy's good luck that the Wind was in one of his kind and helpful moods!

The Wind heard Drippy's frightened cry for help, and he felt sorry for the baby raindrop. He swooped down and picked Drippy up on his coat-tails, carrying him high into the sky. The hummingbird, of course, was furious, but no one can fight the Wind. Not even a hummingbird.

"Who are you?" Drippy asked the Wind.

"Who am I?" the Wind laughed. "Everyone knows who I am."

"I don't," said Drippy rudely. "So you can't be very important."

"I'm the Wind, little raindrop. I blow ships across the ocean. I make waves and tides and make the windmills turn. I blow seeds from flower to flower. Without me, nothing could grow. In fact," he added with a smile, "I'm almost as important as a raindrop."

That was the third time Drippy had heard how important he was -- and even though he still hadn't figured out the reason, he felt very proud of himself.

"Where are your mother and father?" the Wind asked.

Once again, Drippy told his lie.

"I have no family," he said in a sad voice.

"Oh, dear," the Wind said. "Well, never mind," he added kindly. "A lot of special people have no families. I'll take you on an adventure. Would you like that?"

Would Drippy like that! His plump little body shook for joy.

So the Wind picked Drippy up and put him on his coat-tails and took him for a ride in the sky. Higher and higher and higher. It was like riding a giant sled made of wind and star-dust -- all over the big sky.

Drippy and the Wind raced up long hills made of moonbeams and whizzed through dark tunnels of night; just like a train. And the Wind whistled just like a train.

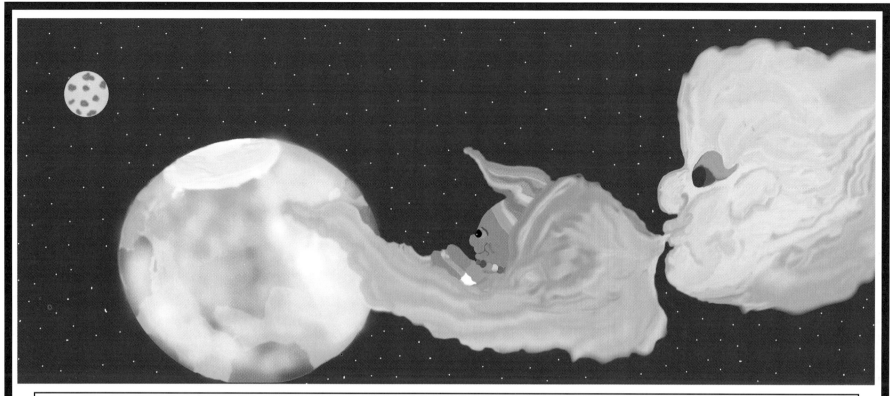

Drippy was having a wonderful time. He looked down and saw the Earth far below. And it looked very tiny. It wasn't, really. But when you are far away from things, they look smaller. Drippy was very far from home. But he didn't care. He was having the most fun he had ever had in his life. And he was such a young raindrop that he didn't know that when you do something that makes someone else sad, it isn't fun anymore.

For far below on the Earth, Drippy's mother, Mrs. Dewdrop, was crying. She had spent all day looking for Drippy, and now she had given up the search. Large beautiful tears rolled out of her eyes and down her cheeks and face. And as the tears moved down, Mrs. Dewdrop moved with them -- for she was made of tears, you see, and in this way she cried herself along the forest glade.

Drippy was much too far away to hear her crying. And he probably wouldn't have cared if he had.

But the Wind has the keenest ears in the world. He heard the sound of the mother raindrop crying, and in an instant he knew the truth.

He realized that Drippy had told him a lie about having no family. He realized that Drippy was a runaway. A runaway who had left home just to have a good time.

And so the Wind decided to punish him.

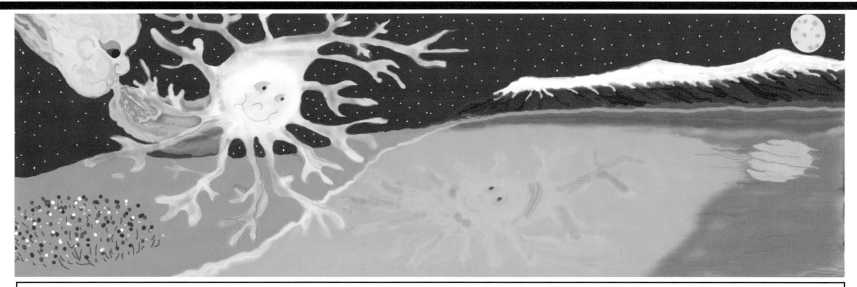

All of a sudden, he turned around and blew Drippy away high into the sky. Higher and higher and higher.

It began to get very cold. And Drippy had no coat. Or hat. Or anything. He began to shiver.

And then something unexpected happened. Drippy started to feel very strange. His body suddenly felt much lighter than it had before. Drippy and the Wind were passing over a lake now, and Drippy looked down and saw his reflection.

He couldn't believe it. He just couldn't believe it. He wasn't a raindrop any longer. He was a snowflake.

A big, wonderful snowflake! He was all white and soft and glistening, and he looked as if he were made of frozen moonlight.

Drippy was overjoyed.

"How beautiful I am."

He had never been a snowflake before, and he was very pleased with himself. *When I was a raindrop,* Drippy thought, *I could only drip. But now that I'm a snowflake, I float!*

Drippy was so happy that he floated all over the skies, dancing here and dancing there, and every time there was a lake or an ocean below him, Drippy stopped to admire his reflection. He could not get over the fact that he was so soft and white and handsome.

"I must be the prettiest snowflake that ever lived," Drippy said.

And the Wind heard him.

He still hasn't learned his lesson, the Wind thought.

And he puffed out his big cheeks and he blew just as hard as he could, and Drippy went tumbling up into the sky higher and higher.

Soon it began to get even colder than it had been before. Colder and colder and colder. And then something remarkable happened. Drippy stopped feeling floaty and light and beautiful. Instead, he began to feel heavy ... and slippery ... and funny. And as he blew by a shining star, he saw a reflection of himself -- and he wasn't a snowflake any more! He was a hailstone. A great big hailstone. Drippy was frozen solid!

Now that Drippy was a hailstone, he was unhappy. He wasn't handsome any more and he couldn't float or dance. But then he took another look at his reflection and he felt better. Because although it was true that he couldn't float or dance, he could bounce.

I'll bet I'm the biggest, bounciest hailstone that ever lived!

Hailstones are bigger and heavier than snowflakes, and Drippy was now so heavy that he began to fall right through the sky, whizzing past the stars and the moon and the clouds, all the way down to Earth.

Kerplunk!

He landed on a sidewalk in a big city, and because he was a  hailstone, he bounced right back into the air, up against a window. It was the window of a house where a family was having dinner.

And he hit the window so hard that he frightened a little boy inside, and the boy began to cry. Drippy was pleased that he was such a brave, scary hailstone.

"Bouncing is fun," Drippy said.

He bounced against everything; horses and cars, and buildings and children, scaring everyone half to death. Drippy had never had such a good time.

He played all night long, running and bouncing, and bouncing and running. But towards morning, he began to get tired. The sky was turning pink and the moon started picking up all the stars and putting them away for the night. And then, all of a sudden, Drippy felt something that he had never felt before. He felt lonely.

There was no one left to play with. The streets were empty. Drippy was all alone. Well, surely his friend the Wind would take him on another adventure.

"I'm ready for some more fun!" Drippy yelled. But there was no reply. The Wind had gone and left him too. There was only the echo of Drippy's voice down the empty streets.

I wish there was someone to play with.

Drippy sat on a curbstone and thought. He thought about all the different creatures he had met in his one day on Earth. He thought about Leapy, who had been so kind and taken him home to breakfast with his family.

He was nice, Drippy thought. *I wish I had been a little nicer back. I wish I had thanked him for his trouble.*

And he thought about the Queen Bee, who had rescued him from the sun and shown him her hive.

She was nice, too, Drippy thought. *And now I'll never see her again. I wish I had thanked her while I had the chance.*

And then Drippy thought of the Wind, who had saved him from the hummingbird, and had taken him on that magical ride through the sky. *And I never said thank you to him either.*

And Drippy started to feel very sad.

It was a strange feeling, because Drippy had never felt sad before. He had only thought about himself and how wonderful he was. But now, all alone, in the middle of a strange city, he started to think about others, and how wonderful *they* had been.

Leapy and the Queen Bee and the Wind had all told him that he was the most important thing in the world.

But Drippy did not feel important. All he felt was miserable and lonely, and very far from home. He bounced against a window and looked inside. A mother was leaning over a crib and covering her baby with a blanket. Seeing them together made a little tear-drop lump come into Drippy's throat. Then he heard voices from the next window, and he bounced over there. Inside the house, a mother and father and three children were having breakfast. *Everyone has someone who cares for them,* Drippy thought. *Everyone except me.*

And then he became so unhappy that he did not think he could stand it a moment longer. For he remembered someone who cared. He remembered his mother. And his father. And his brothers and his sisters and his cousins. And he remembered how he had run away from them.

And Drippy started to cry.
And as he cried, he started to melt; and
pretty soon he was not a hailstone any more.

He was a raindrop again, bright and beautiful and filled with all the colors of the rainbow.

And when the Wind saw this--for of course the Wind had been hiding behind the corner of the building the whole time--when the Wind saw that Drippy had finally learned his lesson, he swooped down and picked the little raindrop up in his arms.

"Where do you want to go?" he asked.

And Drippy said, "Home."

The Wind was very pleased with that answer. Very gently, the Wind carried him all the way back home to the meadow where Drippy had been born, and he blew him right into his mother's arms. And Drippy's mother was so happy, she cried. And then Drippy's father, uncles, aunts and all of his cousins gathered around him and they said, "Tell us about all of your adventures."

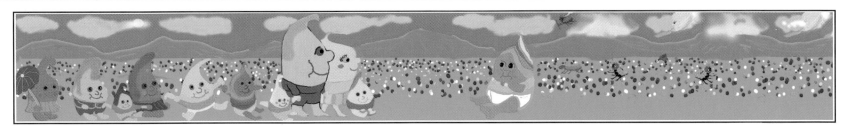

And Drippy looked at them and he thought, *If I tell them all the wonderful things that have happened to me, they'll feel sorry that they didn't happen to them too.*

So Drippy only smiled and shrugged and said, "I didn't have any adventures."

But there was one thing that still bothered Drippy. "The grasshopper, Queen Bee and the Wind all told me that I was the most important thing in the world," Drippy said to his mother and father. "Is that really true?"

"It certainly is," his father told him. "You see, Drippy, you're made of water. And without water, nothing on this Earth can live. Alone, you're just one little drop, Drippy, but when the whole family is together, we keep the whole planet going."

And Drippy nodded happily.

If you ever want to meet Drippy, here's all you have to do. Just go outside when it is raining. You can see him, plump and cute as ever, flowing alongside his mother and his father and his brothers and his sisters and his cousins. He works very hard making the grass grow green and feeding the thirsty flowers and helping the yellow wheat grow tall and strong. Our little

Drippy has turned out to be a fine raindrop.
But as far as his having no new adventures ---
well, he makes no promises.

THE   END